Disney

This magical book belongs to:

Sabina.

DISNEY's
Magical World
of Reading

Peter Pan * Robin Hood

Adapted by Kathryn Knight
Art Direction by Andy Mangrum

Copyright © 2006 by Disney Enterprises, Inc.
All rights reserved.
Published by Dalmatian Press, LLC, in conjunction with Disney Enterprises, Inc.
Printed in China.

14798-1105 Magical World of Reading - Peter Pan and Robin Hood
06 07 08 09 CCO 10 9 8 7 6 5 4 3 2 1

Walt Disney's
Peter Pan

This is a Never Land adventure story, with the boy who never wants to grow up—Peter Pan!

Long ago in London there lived
three children—Wendy, John and Michael.

Wendy liked to tell stories to her brothers.
She told stories about Never Land.
The hero in Never Land was Peter Pan!
Peter Pan was a boy who never grew up.
Peter liked to have adventures!

One night, Peter Pan and Tinker Bell
flew in through the window.
Wendy woke up.
She was so happy to meet Peter Pan!
Peter liked Wendy.
"Fly with me to Never Land," Peter said.
"You never have to grow up there!"
Wendy said, "I'll go, as long as my
brothers can go, too."

So, Peter told Wendy, John
and Michael to think happy thoughts.
Then he sprinkled them with pixie dust.
The pixie dust was magic!

Soon the children were flying!

They flew over the rooftops!

They flew and flew and flew!

Peter led them all the way
to Never Land!

But Tinker Bell did not like Wendy!
Tinker Bell flew to Peter's hideout.
The Lost Boys lived in the hideout.
Tinker Bell told them that a bad
Wendy Bird was flying above them!

When Peter and the children flew by,
the Lost Boys used peashooters to
knock the Wendy Bird out of the sky!

Wendy began to fall.

But Peter flew down.

He caught Wendy!

Peter was mad at Tinker Bell.

He sent her away for a week.

Then Peter took Wendy on a walk

to see the island.

The boys went off on an adventure.
They went through the woods.
And then—oh, my!
They were captured by Indians!

Meanwhile, Peter had taken Wendy
to the beautiful Mermaid Lagoon.

Suddenly, Peter saw a little rowboat.

"It's Captain Hook!" Peter said.

Captain Hook was a pirate.

Peter Pan did not like Captain Hook.

Captain Hook did not like Peter Pan.

Once, Peter had cut off Hook's hand.

The pirate now had a steel hook!

And where did that hand go?
A hungry Crocodile ate it!
The Crocodile liked it so much
that he followed Hook everywhere!
He wanted to eat the rest of him.

Oh, dear! Hook and Mr. Smee had
Tiger Lily, the Indian Princess.
"Tell me where Peter Pan's hideout is,"
Hook said to Tiger lily.
Tiger Lily was Peter's friend.
She did not tell Hook!

Peter flew down
in front of Hook.
They began to fight.
Up and down the cliffs
they went!
Hook slipped—
and the Crocodile snapped!
Mr. Smee pulled Hook into his rowboat.
The Crocodile swam after them!

Peter and Wendy took Tiger Lily home.

The Indian Chief was so happy.

He thanked Peter.

And he let the boys go.

He gave Peter an Indian name:
Little Flying Eagle.

 But Hook was not happy!
He was very mad at Peter Pan.
"Bring me Tinker Bell!" he yelled.

Well, Tinker Bell was still mad at Peter.
That night, she went to Captain Hook.
Hook said, "I need your help.
I need to catch Peter Pan.
Show me where his hideout is."

Tinker Bell dipped her toes in ink.
She danced across a map of Never Land.
Her footprints showed the way
to Peter's hideout.

Hook smiled.
Now he would get Peter Pan
once and for all!
Then he grabbed Tinker Bell
and locked her in a glass lantern!

Back at Peter's hideout,
Wendy told the boys a story.
But they were all very homesick.
"I want my mother," sobbed Michael.
The Lost Boys did not even know
what a mother was.
But they wanted one, too.

Wendy said they would all go back
to her London home together.
Peter did not want to leave Never Land.
He watched sadly as his friends waved good-bye.
"Good-bye, Peter," said Wendy.
"I'll *never* forget you."

But the pirates were waiting for them
just outside the hideout!
The pirates took them to Hook's ship!
"Join my pirate band!" Hook snarled.

The boys wanted to become pirates.
But Wendy did not.
"Peter Pan will save us!" she said.
Hook laughed.
"Peter Pan won't save you this time.
We left a surprise for him—a bomb!"
Oh, no!

Tinker Bell heard these words.

She was in the glass lantern.

She pushed and pushed until—

Crack!

The lantern broke.

Tinker Bell was free!

Tinker Bell flew to Peter's hideout.
He was about to open the present.
She grabbed the box and threw it!
There was a big *bang*!

Tinker Bell told Peter all about
the pirates and the children.
Peter flew off to save them.

Peter Pan was just in time to save
Wendy and the boys!
He turned to fight Captain Hook.
Hook slipped and fell!
Down into the water he went
where the hungry Crocodile waited.

The children clapped and cheered
as Hook swam to Smee's rowboat.
The Crocodile was right behind him!

Tinker Bell sprinkled the ship with pixie dust.
Soon the ship was flying over Never Land.
It flew all the way to London.

Wendy, John and Michael
were happy to be home.
As they waved good-bye,
Peter sailed back to Never Land.

For, Peter Pan, Tinker Bell and the
Lost Boys were not ready to grow up yet.
They were off on another adventure!

Welcome to Sherwood Forest in merry old England, where adventure and laughter await.

Here's the story of a famous hero.
His name is Robin Hood.
He lives in Sherwood Forest
with his band of Merry Men.

One day, a golden carriage
passed by in Sherwood Forest.
But it was not good King Richard.
Good King Richard was away.
This was his brother, Prince John.
And John was not good.

"Hurry," said Robin Hood to his
friend Little John. "I have an idea."
And why was that?
Because Robin Hood was an outlaw!
He stole from the rich
to give to the poor.

"Stop! Stop!" cried a gypsy lady.
"We will tell your fortune!"
Prince John loved to have
his fortune told!
"Will I be rich? Will I?" he asked.

And so, the gypsy lady went into
the carriage to tell his fortune...
....but he stole a sack of gold instead!
Because this was no gypsy woman!
This was Robin Hood!

Prince John was very mad!
"Punish all the people!" he said.
"I want more taxes! More gold!"
He sent his Sheriff to get every coin,
even from the children!

But our hero, Robin Hood,
brought some gold coins
to the poor people.
"Thank you, Robin Hood,"
the children said.

Meanwhile, in the castle,
there lived a pretty lady.
Her name was Maid Marian.
She was in love with Robin Hood.

And Robin Hood was in love with her.
They both dreamed of the day when
good King Richard would return.
Then they could be married.

One day, a grand event took place.
It was called a tournament.
There would be games, and food—
and a Golden Arrow contest!

The best archer in the land
would win a kiss from Maid Marian.
"I'll win that contest!" said Robin.

The day of the contest, the archers
marched past Prince John.
"Hmmm...." thought Maid Marian.
"I think that stork looks like..."
The stork winked at Maid Marian.

Of course, the stork was the best!
Even when the mean Sheriff
tried to mess up the stork's aim...

...he hit the bull's-eye every time!

"You!" cried Prince John.

"You must be Robin Hood!

No other archer could be that good!

Guards! Tie him up!"

But Robin Hood had good friends!
They battled the guards and saved
Robin Hood from Prince John.
"Long live King Richard!"
cried Robin Hood as he scooped up
Maid Marian and went back to the forest.

"Oh, Robin," said Maid Marian,
"you're so brave!"
Robin Hood and Maid Marian
joined all the Merry Men.
They played music and danced
long into the night.

Now Prince John was really mad!
"Put all of Robin's friends in prison!"
he yelled to the Sheriff.

But of course Robin Hood and
Little John came to the rescue!
Robin was good at disguises.

While Little John set everyone free...

...Robin slipped into Prince John's room.

He put up some ropes that led
to the window.

Then he tied bags of gold to the ropes
and sent them down to his friends.

Robin's friends hurried off
with the bags of gold.
"Now the poor will have their
money back," they said.

But Prince John woke up!
Robin tried to escape,
yet what could he do?
Arrows came right at him!

Robin's friends fled from the castle
while the Sheriff set the tower on fire!
But where was Robin?
Would he escape, too?

Yes!

With flames licking at his heels,

Robin leaped from the castle wall!

He escaped into the forest.

Prince John had lost again!

A few days later, Good King Richard
returned to his castle.
All the land was filled with joy!
But who was most joyful?
Why, Robin Hood and Maid Marian
—of course!